<u>Praise for</u>
<u>*A Sasqu...*</u>
<u>*With He...*</u>

"It's somewhere between 'Ulysses' and 'iPad for Dummies'. Closer to the latter though."
—herbalt, *amazon reviewer*

"Anyhoodle, [this book is] frigging hilarious... From the copyright pirate warning, to the chapter headings, to line after line of really funny prose, this short is full of whip-sharp dialogue and clever turns of phrase."
—Acesfull, *amazon reviewer*

<u>Praise for *Lacey Noonan*</u>

"Noonan's back catalogue covers a great deal of ground, and pretty much humps the shit out of it."
—David Roth, *VICE*

"Lacey Noonan has truly catapulted herself, however knowingly, into the pantheons of greatest American authors (F. Scott Fitzgerald, Mark Twain, etc.), greatest female American authors (Willa Cather, Toni Morrison, etc.), and greatest humans (Jesus, Julius Caesar, etc.) to have ever set foot on this great Earth we call home."
—Brenden, *amazon reviewer*

"...one of the literary masters of our time..."
—Jonathan C. Pike, *amazon reviewer*

"She is a very good writer."
—Gary Tricarico, *amazon reviewer*

Praise for *A Gronking to Remember*

"We were made aware this weekend that Gronk erotica exists and is being sold on Amazon. Due journalism diligence insisted we purchase this Gronk erotica, give you a full review, and then turn it into an animated movie."
—*Deadspin*

"'Lacey Noonan,' an author—nay, an American hero—recently penned one of the greatest works of fan fiction we here at Complex Sports had ever seen… We're talking highbrow shit here."
—*Complex*

"It's been a slow year for people who have been looking for NFL-related erotica novels, but the drought is finally over thanks to author Lacey Noonan (Not pictured above)."
—*CBSSports.com*

"Rob Gronkowski might just be the hero that the world of erotica needs right now."
—*Inquisitr.com*

"Rob Gronkowski Erotica Is Here and It's… Something."
—*Boston.com*

"The western canon is scattered with watershed works of literature penned by American authors…add A Gronking to Remember to that list."
—Brenden, *amazon reviewer*

"I don't want to live in a world where this book doesn't exist."
—David B. Hansen, *amazon reviewer*

"Thought this was going to be about the hash browns at Dunkin' Donuts. Disappointing!"
—happykins, *amazon reviewer*

a

The Dishes Are Done Man!

book

Books by *Lacey Noonan*

Novellas

Seduced by the Dad Bod: Book One of the Chill Dad Summer Heat Series

Hot Boxed: How I Found Love on Amazon

The Babysitter Only Rings Once

I Don't Care if My Sasquatch Lover Says the World is Exploding, She's Hot but I'm a Bass Player and There's Nothing Hotter Right Now Than Rap Rock: Book 2 of the …Because It's the New Millennium Series

Eat Fresh: Flo, Jan and Wendy and the Five Dollar Footlong

A Gronking to Remember

A Gronking to Remember 2: Chad Goes Deep in the Neutral Zone

Novels

Shipwrecked on the Island of the She-Gods: A South Pacific Trans Sex Adventure

Collections

The Hotness: Five Burning Hot Novellas

I Don't Care if My Best Friend's Mom is a Sasquatch, She's Hot and I'm Taking a Shower With Her

(...Because It's the New Millennium)

LACEY NOONAN

Copyright © 2015 Lacey Noonan
and The Dishes Are Done, Man!

All rights reserved.
Cover images licensed from Shutterstock.

ISBN: 150758833X
ISBN-13: 978-1507588338

Disclaimer

This is a work of fiction. Any resemblance to actual persons, living or dead, or actual events, except in cases when public figures are being satirized, is purely coincidental. This book is in no way endorsed by any of the public figures mentioned herewith.

CONTENTS

Acknowledgments	i
Chapter 1: *Baby Got Backstory*	3
Chapter 2: *Blast From the Past*	6
Chapter 3: *On the Road*	12
Chapter 4: *I'd Always Been Drawn to the Wild Side*	17
Chapter 5: *What We Have Here Is a Hairy Situation*	26
Chapter 6: *The Titular Line*	31
Chapter 7: *Saxophones & Steam*	36
Chapter 8: *Magical Techniques*	43
Chapter 9: *On the Lam on a Sasquatch*	50
Chapter 10: *Eine Klein Nachtmusik*	54
Chapter 11: *What We Talk About When We Talk About Hoofing It*	65
Chapter 12: *The Road Before Us*	75
About the Author	80
More Books by Lacey Noonan	82

ACKNOWLEDGEMINTS

I would like to thank the following cool, minty treats for helping me on the road to the publication of this novel: York Peppermint Patties, After Eight Thin Mints, Junior Mints, Wintergreen Starlights, Mint Lifesavers, Hershey's Bliss Green Mint Center Chocolate Squares, Bogdon's Mint Reception Candy Sticks, Pearl Couscous Salad with Mint and Pecans, Fatoosh, Zucchini with Mint and Yogurt Spread, Mint Chocolate Chip Ice Cream and last but not leastly, Mint Juleps.

For *Wild People Everywhere*

**I Don't Care If My Best Friend's
Mom is a Sasquatch,
She's Hot and I'm Taking a Shower With Her
...Because It's the New Millennium**

"Sex is a part of nature. I go along with nature."

—*Marilyn Monroe*

Chapter 1
Baby Got Backstory

My best friend Luke's mom was a Sasquatch. She was a Bigfoot, everyone knew that. It was common knowledge in our town. The thing is, no one had ever seen her. We'd hear roars and other strange animal noises coming from inside their house, and as far as we could tell what was what, we'd smell strange animal smells too, but not one of us had ever laid eyes on her.

Naturally, as the years went by, I grew more curious. What the heck could this woman look like? Did she eat raw meat? Did she walk around naked and furry? And how was it that the Lemaire family, Luke, his father and his two older sisters, were all normal human beings? Luke was a shy kid, so I never pressed him on it. Every once in a while when I'd ask if we could go over to his house to play on his Nintendo, he'd get all quiet, look at the ground, toe a few pebbles and say, "Nah, let's not."

"But why?" I'd answer.

He'd breathe a longwinded, longsuffering sigh and say finally, "You know why, Jay. My mom. She's a Sasquatch."

"C'mon, Luke. You have *Zelda II: The Adventure of Link*. All I have is two games, *Super Mario Bros. 3* and *Castlevania II: Simon's Quest*."

"Nah."

After a while, Luke and I drifted apart. It was hard being around him. Kids could be cruel. They'd make fun of him about his mother, and I'd get tossed in the mix, the bully bouillabaisse. I felt bad for abandoning him, but it was a lot to ask of me if you weren't going to include me in on the secret.

Sure, we'd still play every once in a while in the woods, even up through Middle School, throwing old cans at squirrels or arguing about which one of the *Baywatch* babes was the creamiest piece, but that year for Christmas Santa Claus was kind enough to bring me *Zelda II: The Adventure of Link,* and that was it.

Then the next Spring two things happened: a lot of neighborhood cats' and dogs' half-eaten carcasses started appearing in the mornings—and Luke moved away with his family and their mystery to another town. No one knew where. They never called.

Life went on. Operation Desert Shield came and went. Then Operation Desert Storm. I started masturbating regularly. Grunge hit the scene. Rwanda. The Dream Team.

After a while, the whole thing took on the timbre of legend. Just like the mystery of regular Bigfoot, conspiracy theorists and other idiots crowded in. But the saner of us questioned what we knew… Had we made it all up? We thought about it for a second and all came to the same conclusion: *Fuck yes we'd made it up. What a bunch of rubes*, we laughed at ourselves! *Mother a Sasquatch! Ha! Who thought of that?*

Quickly enough, the slaughtered pets and the shy kid from the weird family were forgotten altogether.

Or had they?

Chapter Two
Blast From the Past

Fast-forward ten years.

I'm at a bar and I'm getting my swerve on. A girl has her palm on my thigh. It's causing a bulge in my Hawaiian shorts I'm not embarrassed about. It's that kind of hookup place, seedy. I look at her and smile, she smiles back; we trade smiles through the slimy gauze of Jägermeister and Coors Light. Two drunks ready to split the skins. Either in the graffiti-splooged bathroom in the back, in the back of my car or back at her place. Maybe all three. We have time. It's the new millennium.

"Tammy, where you live, girrrrl?" I slur. "Downtown?"

"Yup" she says with a flirtatious pop of the P. Her hair is magnificently cylindrical, a semi-okay replica of The Rachel, two or three strands of bleached hair curving over her right eyebrow. But she's a full gal. Wide hips. And great breasts press at the front of her pink, low-cut top. She is a drunkard's dream.

Smooth by Santana featuring Rob Thomas trails off and is replaced on the jukebox by Montell Jordan's *Get It On Tonite*—it's groove undeniable, it's directive to freak unquestionable. The mood is tight. Romantic. I put my hand on the hand that is steadily moving up my thigh. "Let's get another round of Jäg' Bombs," I say.

"On ice, pwease."

"Okay, doll. Hey barten—" I stop short. As I rise to get the bartender's attention, I see over Tammy's Rachel something strange that catches my eye. A twinge of memory pecks at my brain. Can it be? Can it really be? "Hey, here's a fiver. I gotta hit the head," I say to Tammy. "Get the shots will ya?"

"Drain the dragon," she says over her shoulder, "but bring it back the way I found it…

chubby, kay?"

"Aight."

I make my way to the back of the bar, smoothing out the front of my pants, smooth, like that Rob Thomas.

But instead of the men's room I go over to the thing I saw. Actually, it's not a thing, but a person.

"Motherfucking bitches in heat, maaaan," the person says. They are alone at their booth, head swaying a few inches above the table, gazing down into their booze, a collection of half-empty pints and shots. "Fucking heated-up bitches, man…" they slur again, and lean back into the light.

Holy shit. "Luke?"

He's older, but it's definitely him. It's my old friend. Same Middle School crew cut and everything. He guides his eyeballs toward me, real slow like an oscillating fan to the voice that has summoned his attention.

"Yeah?" comes the response.

"Holy shit, buddy… It's me, Jay! Jason Fields. Remember me?"

Luke stares at me for a few seconds. His eyes pinching to a squint, eyebrows furrowed. Finally,

I see recognition flutter across his face. He smiles a wide drunken grin. "Jay!" he shouts. "Have a seat, motherfucker!" he shouts again, pounding the table.

I slide in next to him. "Wow," I say, smiling uncontrollably. "How long's it been? A decade?"

"Fucking bitches, man," he says, looking around the bar.

"Yeah. Totally," I laugh.

"Bitches in heat, man."

"Right."

"Fucking bitches in heat, can't deal with 'em…"

"Um."

"Bitches in—"

"You keep saying that. Are you okay? You get dumped?"

"Ah, yeah. Sorry. It's just my father took my sisters to the mountains this weekend and I'm home alone with—" he cuts himself off, looking up at me quickly, or at least as quickly as his drunken eyes can manage, calculating the effect of what he'd said on my face.

Before I could react to this delicious allusion though, Tammy approaches the table with the shots. "Now what the heck are you doing over here, sailor, huh?" she says. God she was a hideous troll, but gorgeous. I'd do her, I thought. Heck, I'd be glad to. Panties down. Bent over the couch. Hands full of Rachel.

"Fucking bitches man!" Luke shouts again.

"What's *his* problem?" says Tammy, scrunching up her face.

"Oh, just drunk as a punk skunk. Got dumped too," I say.

"A dumped drunk pump skump?" Tammy bobbles with her mouth, meeting my eye, trying to maintain our previous connection, coquetry cranked to 11.

I couldn't believe I'd forgotten. I really had. I'd forgotten all about Luke's mother being a Sasquatch. After they left town, I let the memories of everyone thinking we'd made the whole thing up the main memory. Memory does annoying things, it really does. Memory screws the truth in graffiti-splooged bathrooms. Memory throws old cans at squirrels. Memory is the least creamiest piece.

Seeing Luke again had instantly reignited my curiosity. The intervening years had kept the questions boxed up, but I realized then that away from my gaze, the questions had grown in strength. And I realized that I still burned to know what was going on inside his house. Surely Luke was hiding something.

Right then and there I decided to find out the truth.

Chapter Three
On the Road

At that time in my life, being twenty-three, alcohol pretty much cured everything.

So I go with what I know. I go with the flow. And I get Luke superiorly hammered.

I slide Tammy's shot of Jägermeister toward him. Luke picks it up from the table and swallows it in one gulp, slamming the thick-ass glass down with a triumphant turn of his now famous catchphrase, "Bitches in heat, man…"

"Hey! Dickweed!" Tammy yells.

I raise my hand. "Sorry, babe. Do you mind if

I talk to my old friend alone for a bit?" I say to her.

"Fine with me. But you're coming back to my apartment after. Bar's closing in, like, twenty minutes."

"Um, probably not, maybe I can get your number. I'll—"

"My roomie got a little nose candy from Shadebag Sean in the back, though."

"Shadebag Sean? Hmm. Um, nah…"

She gets up quickly, her stool scraping on the floor. "*Whatever.* See you later, *faggot.* Have fun with your *gay*-ass faggoty *boyfriend.*"

Tammy trundles off.

Alone at last. Motioning to the waitress with my hand as I slide *my* Jäger shot at him, I turn to Luke with a glint in my eye… "So just what *the heck* you been up to all these years, buddy?"

Thirty-five minutes and about a dozen rounds of Jägerbombs later (what can I say, I put the Jay in Jägermeister?) I am behind the wheel of Luke's car, an old green Taurus, busting down the road at 80 mph.

He is passed out like a drunk sloth in the back

seat, mumbling, incoherent, on a pile of 100-Hour-Free AOL CD-ROMs that crunch under him every time I take a turn. I weave in and out of traffic. I know this is wrong, but fuck if I care. I'm on a quest. A magic quest befitting Link and Zelda, the royal NES couple themselves.

Luke's wallet is open on the front seat, his ID in my hand. "77 Bourque Road, Raytown. Two towns over. Not a bad place to hide a Sasquatch," I say to the unconscious Luke in the rearview mirror, as I careen down the highway, "Not a bad place at all… you secretive *bastard*."

The car glides to a stop with a jerky, drunken application of breaks in front of Luke's house. It was back aways in the woods, but I can see through the trees it is your standard split-level suburban number. Did the people of this town ever wonder what was hidden inside its walls? Maybe it was far back enough so that any roars or gnarly odoriferous emanations couldn't reach the road. Hey, if this town was ignorant of it all, Luke's family secret was safe with me—if there *was* one, that is.

I turn around and gauge the lump of drunk

friend in the backseat. "Sorry, Luke. But I've got to know."

The driveway is long and gravel. I pull the car gingerly up to the side of the house, shut it off and jump out. Luke's keys are in my hand. I realize my palms are sweating. I'm nervous. This is huge for me. I look at the house.

The place is spooky. A lone light shines through the darkness of the surrounding woods. The trees' shadows long and thin, like skeleton fingers. The sound of crickets and other summery bugs fill the air, a ceaseless droning. Somewhere in the distance a train bleats its lonely horn into the sleeping suburban countryside.

I wobble in place a bit and then it hits me where I am. I can't believe I am actually going to find out, after all these years, what Luke's mother is like. Would everyone back home believe me when I told them?

Booze hums in my ears. I sway a little and take my first step on the walkway towards the house, towards the answer to the great mysterious mystery…

Breaking and entering has never been so easy. Luke's key slides into the front lock, I open the door and step inside…

I don't have to tell you, it was love at first sight.

Chapter Four
I'd Always Been Drawn to the Wild Side

Let me tell you... it was love at first sight.

Love at first sight!

"Good God!" I shout as I walk into the house. The smell is unbelievably pungent and close. Not completely bad, just so intoxicatingly, uncontrollably strong that I fall to one knee as if blackjacked. White filaments and squiggles ghost my vision.

The smell... how to describe it? Like a barn, a greenhouse, an ancient gulch and a strip club all swished together in a bottle. There are high notes of hay and juniper, with a thick base of some kind of perfumy swamp rot.

Before I can assimilate the smell hogging my nasal and skull cavities though, Luke's mother walks into the living room from the dining room. Simply just walks right into the room.

Good God.

I can't believe it. There she is. Her.

It is a miracle of nature.

"Hello," it—*she*—for she certainly *is* a she—says, calmly, plain as day.

It's true! She really is a mythical creature. All these years, the myth was true!

I am aghast, humbled by her presence, which fills the room.

If the smell was intoxicating, the sight of this elegant, enormous sylvan creature is more so. A creature from another time and place, a unique specimen. I realize I was expecting the stereotypical Harry and the Henderson's character. But she is not that *at all*. Not one bit. I quail at the sight of her. She is nearly ten feet tall. And curvaceous. She looms over the room, huge, strong, proud. Simian yes, but so much more than that. There is human intelligence behind her lovely, deep, closely-set black eyes under long eyelashes, a smile playing on her hairy but heart-shaped face. She has full lips. A small, dainty nose. She has dimples. She is naked. She has a slim waist with large, attractively round hips, as if she has worn a girdle off and on over her life. Her large breasts, bigger than the biggest watermelons at the grocery store wiggle under her mat of fur, and she has a darker patch of wool between her long legs, obscuring her genitalia. I find myself thinking what it might look like under her fur, and taking this and her whole presence in at once, I feel my penis in my pants tighten with wonder.

She is truly something.

The female Sasquatch stares at me, ruminating, and rubs her back against the doorjamb slowly.

"You—you… are, like… um, wow," I say.

She growls a bit, hums and makes some ticking noises. Then, to my astonishment, speaks the King's English, enunciating slowly: "Amazing. The first accessible male unit I have seen in the years of my captivity and he is an erudite unit," she chides. Her voice is low, but still feminine. She circles her hefty butt and haunches against the doorjamb now and runs her enormous paws over the front of her thighs. Looking me up and down, she lets out a bass-heavy cooing that shimmies in my loins.

"Well, listen. This is wild for me," I say, stepping closer. "I was a friend of your son's a long time ago and we all heard stories, but I never thought—I mean, we all had pictures of what a Bigfoot looked like. Your son never said anything about you being a *fucking* babe though, seriously."

"Who?"

"Your son… Luke."

"Oh, *him*."

"And you can talk too."

"Listen, come here will you? I cannot come to you. I want to get a better look at you."

That's when I see her ankles are in chains. The heavy chains trail off into the dining room behind her. The dining room is empty of dining gear, the chandelier looking out of place without a table under it. Instead of a table and chairs there is a large open cage, floored with hay and blankets, and a couple buckets—probably one for food and one for water. In places the wallpaper has been scabrously scratched off in long swatches.

They kept her chained up, right in the dining room. That takes hubris and gall.

"Why would they do this to you?" I say. She is

a peaceful creature. A gentle giant. That is obvious to me, with her heart-melting puppy dog eyes, her human feminine-like fullness and docility. They wanted to keep her locked up because they were greedy. Did they really not want to share this beauty with the world? Or was it for her own good? People are cruel assholes and poke things they don't understand with sticks. Suddenly I feel bad about my squirrel-canning days. I want to comfort this creature, I tell myself—not readily admitting that I want more than to just comfort her. Because the truth is, I am attracted to her. She's not human, but she's not *not* human either. She answers a wild, beastly yearning within me that I'd always sensed was there. I can't explain it, but if sexuality is a type of question formed by our innermost psyches and desires, than she is my answer.

I walk to her—a mistake.

Without warning she looses a ferocious growl. She swipes at me with her mighty paw, claws out like knives. Her eyes are blood red, her teeth evil and bared.

I yelp. I leap back, my shirt shredded.

"What the fuck!" I scream, the intoxication dissipating, checking my chest for lacerations.

Luckily there does not appear to be any.

Quickly, her ferocious face subsides back towards a submissive animal. Her head drops. She whimpers. She looks frightened, as if her own actions have frightened her. "Ohhhhhh, I do not mean you harm. I only wish to remove your outer packaging, friend. Can I see your fur?" she asks.

"I don't have any fur."

"Apologies. I mean your… *clothing*. Yes, your clothing. I am sorry. I cannot control my urges. I do not mean to frighten you. Strange as it may seem, *clothing* enrages me. It is my rutting time, you see. I am usually clothed in packaging. They keep me that way and I comply. It is acceptable usually, but not *now*. I am in my time, as I said."

"Is that why you're in chains?"

"Yes. These chains are painful to my hirsute dermis. They exacerbate my agonies."

"Is there any way I can I help you, ma'am?"

"Yes. But your packaging…"

"You mean if I come near you with clothes on you'll hurt me?"

"I do not know."

"If I come to you with clothes on, you'll try to kill me?"

"Not necessarily, but maybe."

I weigh the options. Weird options, really, but options. I want to help her relive the obvious pain she is in as a trapped animal, but she really *is* an animal. I could be a dead-ass naked idiot pretty quickly if I tried to free her in my birthday suit. Or I could walk out the door, never come back, fully clothed. I mean, the mystery had been solved, right? She existed. Did I really need to insert myself into the situation?

Just then a wave of new odors wafts into my nostrils like an aphrodisiac. The room is full with it… It is honey and sugar and jasmine again. Smells of the forest, subtle and fertile, flourishing and comehitherly. I look at her heart-shaped face, her wide, innocent cheeks, and see she is smiling at me again, wondering, wondrous. Does the smell come from her? Somehow this smell and her look answer for me my quandary.

The human heart is broken if it is not in a constant state of being broken. We need to do good things, and we need things that break our heart to get us off our asses and help.

"Better safe than sorry," I say, "right?"

I pull my shredded t-shirt over my head, take off my sneakers one by one and yank off my socks and pull my Hawaiian shorts down, piling them all on the green couch in front of the bay window.

But, my hands on the hem of my boxers, I hesitate.

"Even these?" I ask.

Luke's mother's mouth opens, as if panting. She stares down at the bulge in my boxer shorts from her great height. I follow her gaze to my groin. Wait, where did this erection come from? I am suddenly hot. Her tongue, long and pink, rolls out over her lower lip to her chin. She drools. I feel drawn to her, this beast, this babe, this Venus in Furs and I can't fight it—that's becoming obvious. It feels better to go with the flow. I am at one with the vibe in the room. Fuck it—I slide my boxers down, the hem loop catching the head of my dick. My dick cantilevers down with the boxers and when the boxers are at my knees my dick shoots out and upward like it's on a spring.

Sproi-oi-oi-oing!

My meat thumps against my stomach. At this, Luke's mother jumps up and down as much as she is able to crouched under the low ceiling above her head, and claps her hands. The floor shakes. The whole house groans under her weight. She laughs and I laugh too. She pulls at the chains around her ankles tying to get closer to me, the house creaking against the strain. Her eyes glued to my penis. My penis: rock hard, reaching for the sky.

I'm psyched she's into it.

I feel wild. Not myself. I guess this should have given me pause, but since going to college I'd been drawn to the wild side. I liked to party. I liked pushing the envelope, dipping a toe over the line past my comfort zone, standing next to fires, gleaming the cube. Not being myself is exactly the goal in all this—in all this *life*.

"Well, aren't you a special one?" she says, running her hands over her wide female hips.

"Yes. Yes I am, ma'am."

"Come. Release me." She opens her arms wide.

"Tight. Aight."

And I walk towards her…

Chapter Five
What We Have Here is a Hairy Situation

She does not kill me. Not even a little.

I come up to her, her monstrous girth like a great shaggy altar. Her body is so incredibly huge. Her arms are open wide, a wingspan that nearly reaches both walls of the living room. She purses her lips. She releases a small hoot.

I step into her embrace.

We hug. Her huge, hairy arms envelope me. They are warm, I am hot. We are hot together. I cozy up in her arms, like luxuriating in the warmth of a bearskin rug in front of a fire. Her soft fur is on my naked skin. I am closed in on all sides. Her arms behind me, her warm bosom in front of me. And her breasts rest on the top of my head. I run my fingers through her fur. It is not at all what I expected. It is not the fur of a dog or a cat or any animal I've ever felt. It is more soft than ermine or fox. It is softer than that. Softer than any fur coat. Her fur is unearthly in its feminine softness, angel hair. I tickle it, and in a way, it tickles back. I run my hands along it, through it, like holding your hand out of the window while driving in a car, and her fur rubs me back with its ethereal softness. I entwined my fingers in it, and her fur entwines me deeper into it, as if it had a life of its own.

And her odor inside this enclosure is magnified a million times. Sudden smells can bring you back in time, but instantly here I am hallucinating, shooting back in time a thousand generations before I was born, to a time in North America before humans migrated to it, a deep backwoods piece of Pangaea. My brain warbles in its wooden bucket. My nose is filled with lusty, greenwood wants. I am an acorn, I am a leaf, I am a herd of mammoths crossing a tundra. I am an oak tree, I am growing through the clouds to greet the sun, I am a root system burrowing deep into the earth; I am loam and nutrients.

I begin to rub my groin against her. Sorry, but I can't control myself. I know she was my childhood friend's mom, but I am so ungodly drawn to her. It is a complete attraction, like a complete protein. She is a woman I could fall into. The smell of her sex, not a foot below my head calls unto me in jungle tongues.

"This is nice," I say muffled into her hairy bosom, my fingers twirling in her fur.

"No!" she roars suddenly, "No!" the sound deafening. Her voice is a hurricane, my hair flapping in the wicked wind. "No!"

What have I done?

Fear plunges through me, I nearly pee myself.

"What do you think you're doing?" I hear a voice from outside my womanly enclosure. Her grip loosens around me and I turn to the voice.

"Leave us be!" she shouts.

It's Luke. He's swaying in the doorway. Drunk, barely upright.

Luke jabs a thin piece of metal into his cheek. He does it again, except this time on his other cheek. He looks around, concerned. Then he purses his lips and jabs it into his forehead.

"Luke, what the *fuck* are you doing?" I say.

He brings the piece of metal to his lips—this is apparently what he was trying to do but he was so drunk—and blows in it. All I hear is a puff of wind in the thin metal, but above me, his mother shrieks, so piercingly I plug my ears. Luke has some kind of Sasquatch whistle, the asshole. I run up to him and knock it out of his hand before he can do it again, my shaft flapping free against my body. The whistle flies behind a chair. He wobbles and falls against the door and sinks to his ass on the floor.

"You 'ave nnn idea what you'n doinn'," Luke bumbles from his mouth and proceeds to fall onto his side, passing the fuck out. He gurgles a little. I think he might puke.

"What are you a goddamned freshman? Boot and rally, scrote." I say to the heap on the floor. I turn to his mom. I want back in the hairy house. "Now where were we?"

But I see wildness in her eyes. "Look out!" she screams in her booming voice. I spin around just in time to see Luke raise some contraption at me and press a button.

Instantly I am zapped to death—a beam of light enters my body and a million volts of electricity rattle my bones and seize my muscles. My teeth clench violently in my mouth, squelching a scream. My dong shakes like a tree in a tornado.

Motherfucker tazed me. I pass out.

Chapter Six
The Titular Line

I hear voices. Dark voices, foreign. No, not foreign. They are not human voices.

The voices bring me to. Slowly I become aware of my body. I'm in a crumpled lump, face down ass up on the floor of my childhood friend's living room who I haven't seen in ten years and whose mother I had ever-so-recently become infatuated with and I think the feeling was mutual.

My eyes are pressed against the rug. I hear them talking in their strange language. There are whip sounds. I realize it is Luke whipping his mother. One nasty crack after another. I stay completely still, facing away so he still thinks I'm tazed-out.

At some point, the language switches to English.

"Back! Back in your cage, cur!" It's Luke's voice. This is followed by a whip and whimper from his mother. This enrages me.

"But it is my rutting time. It is time for my daily bath. That is procedure!" she wails.

"Fuck procedure! While the rest of 'em are outta here you can stay fuggin' hot 'n dirty in your cage, bitch!"

Frankly, I am scandalized by all this. Again a whipcrack cuts the air, followed by a wet burp from Luke. He must still be drunk, I think. I need to see what's going on. Slowly, I turn my head towards them.

What I see boils my blood.

Luke's mother is cowering on the precipice to the cage. Luke raises the whip and it comes down harshly on her, slicing into her abdomen. All the hair on her body ripples outward from the impact.

I do not think. I leap to my feet and before Luke sees me I snatch one of the buckets from the floor and slam him on the side of the head with it. For the second time that night Luke crumples on the floor. Or the third time. I can't keep track of all the crumpling.

Luke moans from the floor and holds his head up.

"Quick, hurry!" I yell at his mother, "Where are the keys?"

"In the kitchen there is a keypad. Bring it here, I know the code."

I run into the kitchen. On the counter is something that looks like a remote control. I ran back and hand it up to her. She hits a few buttons, it beeps and the chains around her ankles clink open. She lets out a hefty sigh of relief.

Luke is sitting upright now. Quickly I reach down, take one of the vacant chains and snap it around his neck.

"Wha' th' fuck're you doin' you fuckin' idiot!" he yells, spittle hitting my face. His eyes are half-closed.

"Sorry, man. We were meant to be together. She's your mom, but this is fate, dude. Guess you shoulda let me play *Zelda II* at your crib."

"Zelda crib? The fuck? You're drunk on her pheromones, you shithead! She's in heat. You can't fight it. You're hypnotized. Bitch is'n heat.

You have to be around her for years to fight it."

"Fight it? Why would I want to fight it? I'm *wild*, man. Check out my dick, prick. Hard as a diamond with this diamond dick."

"You're making a huge mistake."

"You made the mistake by keeping this magnificent woman locked away all these years."

His mother, the colossal sexy Sasquatch woman, has been watching this exchange from the corner. With a flash she broadsides Luke with her arm like a ship's boom and he flies back into the cage. I slam the cage door and it locks shut.

"Y-y-you can't do this!" Luke whines, staggering inside the cage. Then he vomits violently and it splashes everywhere. Puke rains over my naked body.

"Oh, I see *you* need a bath as well now, my pet," his mother says.

"My pet! But you're the pet, darling, my sweet pet!"

"It is time for my daily bath. That for which I have been denied."

"So I heard. Do you just lick yourself clean? I mean—no offense, do you?"

"You are a funny one. No. I do not. But *you* can. In the shower. Come with me. There is a facility in the rear of the building structure." She reaches out a paw to me.

"Oh my God, that sounds amazing."

"Don't!" Luke yells. "She's in heat. I'm serious. She's dangerous. You could be killed."

I step to the cage and cover his hands with mine on the bars and look meaningfully into his eyes. Whatever spirit mists my brain, I am still conscious of my dick down below outstretched toward the cage in front of my old friend, but I try not to think about it. "Look, Luke, I don't care if you were my best friend. Your mom's a Sasquatch. She's hot and I'm taking a shower with her. It's the new millennium. Okay?"

"B-but ugh blarch blooooooo—" Luke wobbles, bobbles, pukes and goes down for the count—crumples (another crumple) in the hay and blankets, covered in his upchucked Jägerwaste.

"Come. Bathe with me, my pet," his mother speaks gently to me in her booming, balmy voice.

And I take her outstretched hand…

Chapter Seven
Saxophones & Steam

I acquiesce to her formal beauty.

She takes me by the hand and leads me towards the back of the house, tall, having to duck under the ceiling, emphasizing her simian gait. She is so strong. I probably couldn't have pulled my hand away if I wanted to. But I don't want to. I want her to take me anywhere she wants, to her neverland of enchantment.

I acquiesce to her natural beauty. Her nature's booty.

And the booty. Wow. Two shapely and heaving haunches lead me down a dark hallway through the house. They mesmerize, hypnotize me, one going up, one going down, one going up, one going down, with their shiny fur. I wanted to crawl inside her backside.

Pheromones be damned. Pheromones are real. *This* was real. This was real lust. Animal, low-brained, hypothalamic lust. I find myself bending as I walk too, devolutionary.

We enter a large room off the back of the house. She turns on the light, keeps them dimmed seductively. The room is an oversized bathroom, surely added to the house for just this purpose. There is what looks like a Jacuzzi in the center of the room with frosted glass surrounding it to the ceiling. Hoses lie everywhere.

"Oh, this is going to be so much fun, Homo sapien. I have been longing for this for a long, long timespan. Long have I been imprisoned by this family."

"That's terrible, Mrs. Lemaire," I say, tenderly rubbing my hand along her hip, just above my eyesight.

She engages the faucet and the tub fills with water. She turns to me, suddenly demure. Her left leg glides in front of her right. She bites down on the tip of her thumb. "Do you find me pulchritudinous, male unit?"

I say nothing but walk to her. Walk *into* her.

She grabs me and once again holds me in her arms, enfolding me like a baby in her mother's down. I feel tiny and precious and eminently squeezable. Her grip is a comfort I have not felt in a long time. Her fur velvety against the entire length of my naked body. It feels like home. All my wildness in life has had a purpose it seems—to end with this, this beautiful creature. I nuzzle my head into her soft pillowy fur. She murmurs assent and we begin to gyrate, to rub our bodies together, swaying to the music of the streaming water.

The bathroom fills with steam, intoxicating me more and more.

She picks me up as easily as if I were a doll and steps into the shower with me, closing the door behind us.

I am placed back down on the floor of the tub.

We kiss. There are a dozen showerheads; water rushes over us. This is our first kiss, and my knees turn to butter. Through the emotional intoxication I try to study every moment, to try to remember the caliber and tenor of each microsecond of tongue-twirling and lip-locking for the benefit of future generations.

She holds me up with her strong hands. Never have I felt such romance and wanton lust. Our tongues entwine. Her tongue, huge, like a giant piece of uncooked liver, runs around my whole mouth, and shoots down my throat. I open my mouth wider to accept her. I let her invade my throat—it tickles and thrusts deep, down, way down, but I do not choke. I grip her fur and hold on, feeling all the powerful emotions.

She removes her tongue. We soap each other's bodies and rub up and down one another. Lube-Factor Eleven. She carefully washes away her son's vomit from my skin, and I lather her up real good, stroking her fur, washing, conditioning, rinsing, repeating.

"This is a tradition going back untold generations," she intones. "Of great importance. The bathing of female components in their time."

"Am I doing it right?"

"Oh, it is very hard to do wrong, human male component. Here…" she runs her paws down my body, her fingers each its own luffa. She scrubs my back, my buttocks, my hamstrings and my calves. She spins me around and laves my testicles and my penis, my taint, my armpits, behind my ears, all the heavenly spots. I tingle beautifully, sparklingly, like my body is a galaxy of twinkling stars.

"Mrs. Lemaire?"

"Yes my, pet?"

"Why do you do it? Why do you need to bathe?"

"It is simple. Overheating. Cleanliness is highly important of course as well, but you saw me out there. How ferocious I was. It was the heat inside me. My homeland is much cooler. Here, your clime is incredibly hot. It is why I have fur, to protect against the heat. It is true, I am dangerous, as he said. But not in here, not in the bath. I do have lust I must admit, here with you, but in here it is sensual—not homicidal."

"That's wild. That's wet *and* wild," I say.

We kiss again. I was and am so hot I never realized that the water had changed from hot to cool. I was so fired up I didn't even notice.

Soft music begins to play in the bathroom. It wafts down from unseen speakers. Saxophones and DX7 keyboards. Ethereal conjuring weirdness. A melted pink space jazz, smooth. A thousand times smoother than Santana featuring Rob Thomas.

Mrs. Lemaire raises her head from our kiss, her tongue emptying out of my mouth. "Ah, the song of my people," she whispers into the cascade of water.

"Beautiful," I say, "just like you, my pet." The music bathes us as we continue to bathe each other.

"Thank you... you... what is your name, my pet?"

"Jay. Jason."

"Jay Jason," she says, running her hands the length of my body, just above my stomach, then squeezes my sides, forcing my cock to protrude further out. Her eyes bulge staring at it. I long for her to touch it, to unleash that vicious tongue of hers, to grip it like hands on an ice cream cone, but I'm too scared to ask, to step out of place. I am desperate for her to suck me off with those great fleshy lips and long slithery tongue of hers, but there is a ceremony here I wish to adhere to. I tremble.

"What is your name?" I ask, nervous, horny, squeezed.

"It is unpronounceable in your tongue."

"Try me. I've gotten pretty used to your tongue so far, after all, ha ha. I think you're beautiful. I bet your name is too. I want to hear it."

"Accepted. Prepare yourself."

She steps back in the water and before I know what the hell is going on she unleashes a howling screech of syllables that rolls into my brain like the ululating war chant of a million savages. Jet fighters, lightning bolts, galaxies colliding.

I wobble on my feet. And I am in danger of perpetrating the night's umpteenth crumpling.

Chapter Eight
Magical Techniques

I crash down, splashing into the tub, touching down like the Apollo Command Module in the middle of the bright blue ocean. I am dazed. My head ringing. The water is well past my hips, but only to her ankles. The head of my penis floats above the surface like an island. I stare at the island, wonder what it means.

"My human pet," she says, "Are you injured? It is the name my people have given me. I am regretful I have said it in such close proximity to you. It needs be uttered in wide open spaces—on plains, across oceans, in space."

I shake the pain out of my ears. "That's a hell

of a name, Mrs. Lemaire." I look up at her immensity from the floor of the tub—she is even bigger from down here, more magnificent, her slim figure, her wide hips, he protruding breasts the size of exercise balls, all slick with water. My island rises higher from its watery grave like a leviathan, eager to conquer her continent.

"Translated to your tongue it means something akin to 'Flower Stem of Starlight.'"

I was still messed up from hearing the name in her howler monkey language. The English version—I only heard the end—I hear as "Starla."

"Starla," I say. "That is a pretty name."

She releases a surprised series of simian hoots and hauls me out of the water under my armpits. She presses my naked, wet body into hers.

"Starla. I like that. Oh, call me Starla. Starla… I have never possessed a first name before! Your eponymy skills are inimitable!" she exclaims and squeezes me tighter, squeezing the very breath out of me.

Starla lifts me up to where we're eye to eye and we kiss anew, locking lips.

Again, I wade into her passion and meld with her. My feet dangle in the air. Water washes over us and drips from my toes into the tub. I free my hands and make way for her breasts, two hairy globes I long to touch. I want to bring this creature unholy amounts of pleasure. I go for what I know. Sifting through her fur, I locate first one, then the other nipple.

These nipples. Wow. As big as rubber balls on their own. I palm them and circle my hands around them.

Starla purrs into my mouth and the tongue unfurls again, splits my lips apart, forces its way in. I open my mouth to receive her. I close my eyes in the passion field.

Still holding me aloft, Starla takes a hand off my head and trails it down my body. I begin to tremble. I yearn for her touch. For the touch that will release me. That will join me to her.

Her hands are smooth but have rough pads on the fingertips. As she explores my body it feels as if she is exfoliating and massaging my flesh at the same time. She runs her hand down my chest and to my stomach, squeezing my muscles, tracing the shape of me. She pulls my arms away from her breasts and up over my head. I let her. She lets go and I hold them up over me. I want to be this exposed.

Then her arm falls and it encircles my penis.

My dick is incredibly hard, nearly purple with pleasure. She squeezes gently and begins to run her hand up and down my shaft between her soapy fingers.

My arms above me, my psyche is quickly becoming one with the urges in the member that juts out of my body at a ninety degree angle toward my lover. I feel like a human male penis.

She begins to work me.

My cock and balls slippery with soap and water, I groan. My hands fall to my sides, pleasure-feeble.

Then two very strange things happen at once. Two incredibly sexy things—but strange nonetheless.

Starla moves in for another kiss, and I open my mouth, but instead of meeting lips, she opens her mouth incredibly wide and swallows my head. My entire head is inside her mouth.

This is new, I think.

Dark, damp and hot—my head *inside* hers. Her tongue swirls around my face, my eye sockets, my forehead, under my chin. I am thoroughly enclosed by her. If there was any cause for fear in all this, it is immediately assuaged by the other strange and sexy thing that happens: Her fur itself begins to caress me.

"Oh my God. Your... your *fur*. It's doing things to me..." I say inside her mouth.

"Go with it, my pet," she rumbles into my head.

"It's freaking me out kinda."

"Relaaaaaax..."

"It's freaking me out, but I'm freaking out in a good way. It's wild, for sure. Fur sure!"

Underneath my bottom, her hair swirls on my skin like smoke along a floor. With her hand on my manhood, the fur traces my body, tickling me in all my private places. The pleasure rises immensely, my dick goes rock hard in her hand, which she had been steadily stroking while cupping my balls.

Her hair has a mind of its own. I wasn't making that up before when I felt it back in the front of the house. It is magical. It weaves itself around my legs and up inside my buttcheeks. It tickles, yes, but shoots lasers and waves of naughty pleasure into my body. I had never been touched in so many places at once by a woman. I am becoming a thing of pleasure.

Meanwhile, my head inside hers, her slobber coats my face. She begins to suck on my head as if giving it a blowjob. She is literally giving my head head. Up and down, down and out and back in again, my face goes in and out of her puckered lips.

"Oh my God," I whisper as my head exits hers and goes back in, covered in slobber. She sucks on me like a lollipop. I feel like sexy food. I feel like edible underwear or something, drenched in Sasquatch saliva.

I reach out to touch her. I can't see anything, but I know where she is. I feel her heat on me. I reach and my hands meet fur and the fur meets me back. As if guided by a spirit, her fur guides my hands down, down to her breasts, wet and soft and warm like the body of a porpoise. I run my hands back and forth, focusing on the nipples. Starla moans into my head. The slobber begins to run out and over my whole body, only to be washed away by the many shower heads—the hundred-headed hydra of the Jacuzzi-Sasquatch-washing-and-sound-system the Lemaires had installed for just this porpoise.

"Oh my God," I whisper again, as she blowjobs my head out of hers on the downstroke. "Honey pet, you're going to make me come…"

"Good," she says. "I do so enjoy the human

male organ. That's it, yes, hump your hips for me, for your sexy mama. That's right. Pump yourself into my hand."

"Like this?" I say and begin to sway my hips, and the fur guides me, as if she is leading me in a dance. Back and forth, front to back. Starla grips my erection, her fur cups my ass and my head slides in and out of her mouth.

"I'm going to… I'm going…" I stutter. Starla is bringing me to orgasm. It is a gift. Its hugeness looms before me. My balls are aching something fierce. She is a master at this. She is a superior sex goddess.

"Come for me," she says again. "That's right." She strokes faster now. Stronger, her strong capable hands conforming to my shape, to my shaft. My consciousness goes real small as the orgasm swells in my cock. Any second now…

"Oh!" I shout, gorgeous in my flesh, "Oh, here it c—"

Luke busts into the bathroom, whips open the shower door and shoots me with the tazer again.

Chapter Nine
On the Lam On a Sasquatch

For the second time that night, I awake a mess, naked, lost, throttled, angular. As my brain grumpily reboots, I realize how tiresome it is, with the vantage of twice in less than thirty minutes, of the whole rigmarole of the cycle of consciousness and unconsciousness, of sleeping and waking. Better to just live forty years and never sleep. All this time wasted in the nether land of *about to be* wake, *about to* sleep. Och, don't even talk to me about it.

This time though I awake in darkness, a sensation of bounding calling me back to the land of the living, in the furry arms of my beloved.

She is running. I can tell by the cool air finding me in my simian love hut that we are outside.

I reach up and touch her face. "It's like I've lived my whole life just to meet you," I murmur.

"Hush, now, human male pet. My word, I forgot what the woods felt like. Here I am free."

"But I want to tell the whole world."

"We are almost there."

"Don't you think we're just the cat's pajamas together though, Starla?"

"I believe that is what you humans call Fate."

"Boy, you are a *smart* Big Foot, Star."

She grunts, a tone of disapproval.

"Oh, I'm sorry. I didn't mean to…"

"There are things you need to learn about me. You need to know the whole truth if you are to be with me as my mate. Things you may not appreciate, for the scales will fall from your eyes and the truth will be shown. Then, and only then, may you profess your adulations."

I take all this in. I nuzzle into her body, comfortable for now in her female strength. "Okay, then." My brain is still frazzled, I can't possibly calculate future worries. We run some more. Bounding up and down. We're in the trees. Suburban trees. Houses a hundred yards apart in every direction, separated by woods. "How did we get here?"

"We are not there yet. We are almost there, pet."

"I mean, what happened back in the shower?" I reach into her soft down and pinch her. She giggles, breaks her stride for half a step.

"Do not do that!"

"Why won't you tell me? Did you kill Luke?"

"Heavens, no! The idiot male unit fell unconscious of his own accord once again. I merely punctured a hole in the wall and absconded with you, my beloved pet."

"Phew."

"You would not express utterances of relief if you knew the truth of his people."

"I know. I saw the whip. Nasty shit."

"Oh, the whip I rather like. Hush now, we are almost there. You will need to prepare yourself for me once again." And she arches her head down and licks my face.

I laugh. My erection stirs. If I had blue balls from before in the shower, Luke's tazer has zapped it clean. "Where? Where are we going, Star?"

She leaps over a fallen log, ducks down under

a low-hanging branch. We run through the backyard of a house. A dog barks. Crickets chirp. We enter the woods again through a bower. Her feet crunch on the dead leaves below. I nuzzle in once again, arranging my body for the long haul. Who knows where we're going? Mt. Rainier? The outskirts of Yellowknife, Northern Territories? But she stops running and stands up straight.

"We are here."

Well.

Chapter Ten
Eine Klein Nachtmusik

I look at her pretty face in the darkness. "But we're still in the woods," I say, confused.

"No, look."

I sit up in my VIP box. In front of us there is a pond. A secluded little lake in the woods. Moonlight reflects softly on its surface, lightly rippling. Before I can remark further she steps into it, loosing a long sigh of relief. "Ahh, the coolness," she says.

She descends into the pond, me with her. My hairy home fills with water.

The water really does feel good. She lets me go and we part. She dives under. I do the same. It is as cool and refreshing as a glass of my sweet, sweet Jägermeister.

I come up and see that she has come up too, at the far end of the pond.

"What are you doing way over there?" I yell across the water. My voice echoes around the amphitheater of the surrounding trees and through the woods.

"Shush, my pet!" she whispers—and I hear her completely fine. What can I say? I am still drunk. Exhilarated by recent events. Indoor voice is beyond me.

Across the pond, Starla dives back under the surface. Within seconds she rises before me.

The moonlight, the water, the suburban night sky, the orchestra of stars twinkling above, and a hairy hefty sexy mama… Passion fills my heart. The moonlight is in her eyes, two smaller ponds of black light. She smiles and we reach for one another.

We embrace again. Entwining, kissing, adding our heat together in the cool bath of the surprising woodsy pond.

Underneath the water she begins to kick her legs and we move slowly in circles. We kiss and we dance a synchronized pattern. Our hands rove each other, exploring the landscapes of each other's bodies. We are free from the house, I realize. Outside. On our own, miles away from her prison. We can do as we please without fear of Luke and his idiot tazer. Starla French kisses me again, her tongue fatly filling my mouth, then sliding down my throat.

As far as I can reach while locked to her tongue-wise, my hands slide down Starla's front, from her heaving breasts, to her flat stomach, down to her wide hips and between her legs.

"Oh, human," she says. I see her smile in the moonlight, her eyes closing halfway.

My fingers circle around on the tufts of hair down there. What will I find? I don't know. This is no common Tammy.

My fingers search the soft fluffy area. I reach down further, further...

It's too far. I have to go underwater. I remove myself from her kiss, her tongue uncoils out, I suck in a gulp of air and go under. This way, though, I can use two hands. I latch my legs around one of hers, thicker than a telephone pole. Without benefit of sight, I explore the area between her hips. Even underwater the hair is soft and light. I go down, further, and find a soft bump, maybe her clitoris. I flick it gently with the tips of my fingers—above I hear her hum—it vibrates through the water.

I'm on the right track.

Now her fur comes alive again. I forgot about that. I will have to ask her. The fur elongates as if by magic, takes hold of my fingers and brings them lower—to a place wetter than the water. I touch soft, slick, hairless folds—these must be her bestial female lips. I run my fingers up and down them with the help of Starla's own magical pubic hair.

Vibrations surround me, buffet me underwater. Starla is shaking. It's turning her on. My erection displaces more water. The vibrations are stronger now. I am like a submarine attacked by depth charges. I hold on tight.

But am I running out of air. Actually, I have none. My brains begins to go black. I can't take my hand away—the hair is holding me underwater. I thrash around. Start to panic. I pedal my legs frantically.

With what little air is left in my lungs, I shout for help.

Sensing this, the hair that was guiding me in the ways of pleasuring its master passes me upward. From pubic hair, to stomach and breast hair. Quickly I break the surface.

Air!

"Woooahhhwoweee!" I yell into the sky. Water splashes everywhere.

Starla covers my mouth. I inhale strongly through my nose. "You have got to be quiet, sweet pet. We are far from the family domicile, but they have cunning devices with which to hear."

"Sorry. I got carried away."

"I know… I *felt* it."

"Did you like it?"

"Oh, *yes*."

"It's hard to get there, though. I can only do so much. Let's get on dry land. I want to be inside you right now so much it hurts."

"It is true. Our physiognomies present certain difficulties."

"Okay. Let's get out."

"No. Wait. Watch."

Starla pushes off me and floats on her back. Her strength is such that within a moment she is a hundred feet away. She gently works her feet, turns around and swims back to me, like a paddleboat.

I'm not sure what she's doing, but as she swiftly glides by, she picks me up and places me on top of her. She is like a raft, wide and soft.

We laugh together under the admiring stars. I crawl on my stomach up and over the ramparts of her breasts, coming down on the other side. I reach for a kiss, but something is holding me back. I look down and realize my cock is between her breasts. She sees what is happening and reaches with her great paws, squeezing each tit together, and traps my dick between them.

"Penetrate my breasts, Jay Jason. Please. Do as you wish to me."

I slowly hump her lovely mounds. "But I want to make you happy," I say. "I'd rather do you... down there."

She releases a moan to the dark violet galaxies in the black sky. "This is good, here. Yes, keep doing that. Yes, back and forth."

I raise myself up on her shoulders and begin pumping away. Soon my cock is rock hard. Her fur forms a tube around it. Her breasts feel amazing.

"Squirt on my face, I command it," she says. "Release yourself onto my visage, male unit."

"I want to come *inside* you, baby. Fuck..." I

say, but keep humping her massive chest.

"That is acceptable, also." But her tongue escapes from her mouth, and as I slide in and out of her lovely, gigantic mounds, she flicks it at the head of my cock—little love whips with her tongue that send shivers of joy up my back. Yeah, I guess whipping can be good, like she said, I think.

"Oh God, Sasquatch mama… I'm gonna shoot my load."

Heat consumes me. Lust takes me. Her perfume overpowers the pond and fills my nose with desire. The hairs on my neck stand on end. My back arches. I pump harder and faster, lustily.

But this is beastly lust. Wolves and bison migrate up my central nervous system. This is natural selection lust. Primal, inescapable. Survival of the ferocious. Pine cones falling from trees over eons. You don't survive to the next round by titty fucking. You have to pound the box.

I escape out from her mountains, heading southward, letting the soft sensitive part of my dick glide along her soft fur. As I do so, the fur reaches out to my dick, holding it aloft, as if crowd surfing, or supplicants reaching for a saint, tending fingers fondling.

My legs go out into the water, hanging off my fluffy raft, but I stay atop her. My cock knows where to go. She spreads her legs.

Starla begins to hum a tune as she floats under me. It is soft and jazzy, like the keyboards and saxophones from the bath before. It is a music before time. As my member gets closer to where it needs to go the tune grows in melody. More notes, all over the place. It is a lullaby. A moonlit serenade. A little night music. She is calling to the universe above.

I reach my hand down under the dark wooly patch over her crotch. It does not take me long to find what I'm looking for. With both hands now I stroke her oversized clitoris, and along the folds of her Sasquatch pussy. Her melody takes an uncertain jump and pause—I know where I'm supposed to be. Starla spreads her legs more. Her scent reaches my nose and again I am beyond intoxicated. My vision swirls, and the red lust explodes ten fold in me. I can wait no further…

Still afloat—she is marvelously afloat—a flotilla of sexy beast spread wide across the pond, I enter her. I jam my dick in her Sasquatch vagina. Starla moans, her song takes a stratospheric turn, whizzing high notes, beyond what I thought her baritone could reach.

If there was any doubt in my mind as to how this would work, it disappears from my head...

"Wow, Starla. I thought I would be way too small for you..."

"No. You are so big, human male unit. Your genitalia is stretching my genitals wide. The pleasure is immense. It is too big. I can barely take you in. Now... how do you say... Fuck me? Fuck me, Jay Jason. Fuck your Starla like it is your last night on Earth." She says all this in a strange whispering combination of speech and song.

But it's true. Her pussy is tight, it grips my cock. However this sweet creature evolved, evolution saw to it to give her parts that would satisfy a human man. And I begin to seriously fuck her now. My hands hold on for dear life, wrapped in the fur on her stomach as I fuck this creature of the forest. The wildness of it all, my balls—dropping in and out of the water with each thrust—are singing with it, with Starla's song, with the whole wild, beastly night.

Starla circles around the pond as I pound into her. The song turns into animal shrieks. She growls and howls. We buck as I pound into my sweet life raft. The soft moonlight on the surface of the pond shatters with the waves we are creating. It is still a moonlight serenade, adagio, but full aggro. She raises her hips to meet me as I pound into her tight box.

I see shudders of pleasure take over her body. Her eyes close fully. She is breathing heavy, wildly. Her massive strength dwindles away with each loving stroke. She softens.

I'm afraid of capsizing, but I continue on, a buck-naked sailor humping this great big humpback whale of a woman in a suburban pond.

"Starla, I don't think I can stop myself any more. I need to come inside you. Are you… you… Are you close?"

She breaks through her wailing to answer, "close to what?"

"To coming. To your orgasm? Do you know what an orgasm is?"

"Yes, incredibly close. Five more thrusts with your human male meat, Jay Jason. That is all I require with—Ah ah!"

"Yessssssss…"

"Yes, dig out my tiny hole. Oh, you are ramming me good. Tell me you are ramming me with all your strength. You are melting me."

"I'm ramming you."

"Yes."

"Soothing your savage soul…"

"Yes!"

I have already fucked in and out of her three times. Then the fourth time comes quick. I feel an earthquake summoning in my testicles. The rocket launch is imminent. My back arches violently, and my hips shake incessantly. My load feels like it's being sucked from every part of my body, as if I were made of jizz and the jizz is being drained completely. I am about to be emptied out. My eyes roll in the back of my head.

And that's it. In the micro-moment before my one last thrust, we meet eyes in the sultry moonlight. I see in hers the untold story of the ancient woods, of sentient mountains, deep knowing rivers. I see ages and eons.

We both gasp.

I shoot my hot load into her tight, wet pussy.

Chapter Eleven
What We Talk About When We Talk About Hoofing It

Starla's moans of ecstasy fill the tiny bowl of pond cupped in the woods. They reach up to the night sky like hot smoke from a fire. Sitting astride her, I shake with uncontrollable pleasure, and it as if the entire universe is shaking with our orgasms. The stars jiggle. The moon melts into its own light in the sky. It is like riding a bucking stallion. If her fur itself did not wrap around my wrists to hold me down, I might have flown off her, cannonballing into the pond dozens of yards away. Her breasts—two wild beanbag chairs filled with silicone—bound up and down violently, ram into me.

Then I hear the tone she used when she told me her name in the shower—the strident painful yowling like audible knives. It shoots into my ears. My hands fly up, trying to block the sound.

I look at Starla floating under me on the water. Her eyes are wide open, startled. So soon after our nature-melting orgasm? Is this part of it for her? Starla jumps up, stands in the pond. Instinctively, she pulls me to her hip, like a mother holds a toddler. Her ears perk up, she sniffs the wind. I feel the tension in her muscles. I am afraid.

"What is—"

"Hush," she says, and puts a hand to my lips.

Then the sound bombards the air again, rifling through the trees, filling the woods with awfulness. It is the same ululating, howling screech as before... Only it wasn't from Starla.

"Oh no!" Starla yells.

"What?"

She does not answer, only runs for the shore of the pond in the opposite direction of the sound, her movement slow against the deep water.

I press my head into her fur. Only moments before we were copulating, making love floating in a pond under beautiful, tender moonlight. Now we were running again. Running from what?

Light fills the woods. I turn to it behind us, trying to see. Something whizzes by overhead, and beyond us, a tree explodes like a firework. Then another and another. Starla leaps out of the water and immediately ducks—a beam of light just misses her. She turns to the light and lets out a violent roar, quivering the surface of the pond and shaking the trees and everything around us and also my loins which, if I'm being completely honest, isn't altogether unpleasant. It's like, louder than Lollapalooza.

"They are calling my name. It was a mistake to come here. I should have gone further."

"Who?"

"I was so attracted to you my pet I stopped at the first watering place. And my voluble vociferations of pleasure alerted them."

"Alerted who?"

Across the expanse of woods and across the lake I see people move in front of the light. One of them lets out another simian shriek that finds its way to the most sensitive parts of my inner ear.

Starla shivers, looks down at me. "It is my family. All of them."

"What should we do?"

"Run."

Starla turns and bounds into the blackness. The blasts of light resume around us, nearly hitting us. They make two or three howls too that rocket across the pond. I am starting to be able to differentiate them now. I can tell they are made by different people.

"But how are they doing that?" I ask, thinking out loud. "They're regular people."

Starla leaps over a small ravine. She lands and grunts. I feel the shock through her body.

"They are not regular people, pet," she yells, breathing hard as she runs.

"I always thought Luke was weird!"

"You don't know the half of it. We have to get away from them. There is no telling what they will do. Punishment, affirmative for me. But you? That is a quandary. I do not know what they will do now that you have seen me and have performed sexual intercourse upon me. Possibly resulting in a violent end for you, human male unit."

Panic throttles my voice. It is high and weak and lispy and I don't care: "What if I just go back home and you go home and we can forget this ever happened?" I squeak out, a total puss.

"Negative. They will find you. You are not safe anywhere. They have ways to track you down anywhere on Earth."

"But where can we go that we won't be seen? Where the hell can we *possibly* fit in? A circus?"

"I must take us back to my homeland."

"Really?"

"There you will be safe. I am sure of it."

"Oh God!" I cry, bereaved. What have I gotten myself into?

Finally we come to a road. Empty in both directions. No houses in sight. Starla bounds across it and down the other side into a ravine. She crouches behind a bush.

"What are we waiting for, Starla? Shouldn't we be hoofing it to Yellowknife or Mt. Rainier or wherever you're from?"

"Keep quiet!" she whispers. "Hoof? You think I have hooves, Jay Jayson?"

"No! It's an expression."

"Oh yes, human expressions. I know them well. I will inculcate that one. Thank you. In response to your question, I am waiting for locomotion. Where we are going is much further than I am willing or able to carry you, sweetened one."

I nuzzle into her shoulder, inhaling her musky perfume deeply. I'm starting to get cranky from staying up so late. Then I realize something… "Holy shit, farther than Yellowknife? That's like five thousand miles from here."

"Much further than that."

"Like Asia? Look," I say, "are you a Yeti? You have to tell me if you are."

"Shush! Look now!"

I peer over her hairy shoulder down the road. I see a lone light making its way toward us. A motorcycle. Before I know it, the bike is upon us. Starla drops me to the ground and leaps out into the middle of the road, sticks out her airplane wing arms and roars at the oncoming traffic.

With a squeal of brakes and skidding, the motorcycle enthusiast responds the way any normal human would. He falls over trying to avoid a collision with her, skating on the side of the bike a hundred feet, laying down a thick shower of sparks. The bike comes to a stop right in front of her and the biker pops up and runs back down the road in the opposite direction, screaming bloody murder.

Starla picks up the motorcycle, a Yamaha crotch rocket. It is white and neon green and blue. She steps her leg over it. She looks like an adult on a kid's tiny bicycle but she manages the controls, revs the engine.

She looks over at me—a shivering naked boy in the dark by the side of the road. "Well?" she asks, her voice low and voluptuous.

"Well what?"

"Climb upon my posterior, human male unit."

"Look, I think I want to go home."

She holds out her long arm to me, almost reaching me from the middle of the road. I don't move. Just stare at her. She is beautiful, there is no denying that. Bending over the bike as she does accentuates the form of her ass and I feel my naked dick down in the dark perk up again. I really am smitten with this kitten. But what could possibly come of it? I'd been wild, that was the important thing. I could check this particular adventure off my bucket list and move onto the next. Maybe parasailing in Florida, or following Phish next summer, or rollerblading the Appalachian Trail.

"Please, there is *little* time," she says.

"Just go," I say, tears welling up in my eyes. "Save yourself. I'll only slow you down."

She revs the engine again, looks at me, her ears tuned to the forest. "Please, my pet," she says, emotion crawling into her voice. "Please," she says again, lower, sadness overtaking her now, "I know where to go that is safe for us."

"Just go. I don't give a shit any more. I'm done. What would I do in your homeland anyway?"

Starla looks at me and thinks for a moment. She chews at her lip. "Have it your way. They are going to find you though."

"I'll manage, okay? I always do. I'm wild."

"You are, Jay Jason. You are wild. But you better hoof it to wherever you need to go. Instantly."

She puts one foot up on the bike, revs the motor something fierce. "Good-bye, my pet," she says, and I see the crotch rocket light reflect on a tear that slides from her eye and down her soft downy cheek.

Then the motorcycle screams under her and she takes off down the road, zero to sixty in two seconds. The light recedes and in a mile the road bends around a stand of trees and she is gone, the whine of the bike evaporating into the cool night air.

I am insensate. Crying like a baby. Also, naked as one.

But I don't have time to be philosophical, to catalog my 96 tears, because from the other direction on the road I see a car speeding toward me. It's at least two miles down the road, but I can tell it's a pickup truck. And it's going fast. Something about it is not right. Then I hear it.

From the truck, a ululating simian howl is unleashed down the road at me. It shoots directly into my ears and assaults my brain, jabs knives into my cerebellum.

It is the Lemaire family. They're after Starla.

Within seconds the truck comes upon me. It is about a hundred feet away. Before I realize what I'm doing, I step out onto the edge of the road. I wave my arms like a maniac and shout, "Hey! Hey! Over here!" If I can slow them down just a little bit, I think, maybe Starla can get away.

The truck blasts past me, but I see they see me. One of Luke's sisters is driving the truck, his father is in the passenger seat, his head out the window, holding a long silver rifle. The dashboard lights glow on their dead, humorless faces.

The other sister is standing up in the back. She has a silver rifle too, leaning forward over the roof. Luke, probably still feeling the Jägers like a total fucking scrote sophomore, I see is sitting down, his back against the window of the cab, his face green.

They blow by me, but the truck skids to a stop, violently. I hear it switching gears—does a quick three point turn.

Now the truck is pointed at me and Luke's sister puts the truck in drive.

"Uh-oh."

Chapter Twelve
The Road Before Us

My stomach scrunches to a tight ball of twine in my stomach. I bolt down the road. Foot over foot over foot.

The truck engine wails and I hear the peeling of tires on the blacktop. Without running sneakers I am not faster than a truck. This is just true. And this truth is going to be a problem. A bullet screams over my shoulder and blows a pothole out of the road in front of me in an explosion of sparks.

"Fuck, let 'em kill me," I say, seeing this and slowing down, but still jogging. I'm already winded. I'd rather die than have to run when I'm tired and wasted after a night of proper shagging.

I'm ready to give up. But then I hear it.

I turn my head and see another light behind the truck, a half a mile back, moving toward us at ungodly speed. It is a motorcycle…

My heart leaps in my chest. "Come and get me you fucking fuckers!" I yell at the truck. "Your mother wears combat boots!" I turn and sprint now, as fast as I can. My man-meat whaps against my body with every stride, and it hurts, it is sore from the night's gymnastics, but I pay it no mind. I put my muscles to use. I run.

More blasts erupt on the road around me. I turn and see the motorcycle—a huge, dark shape astride it—and is almost at the truck now.

And the truck is at my heels. The headlights blare on the road in front of me, my shadow long. I turn one last time to see Luke's sister pointing her silver rifle directly at me… The motorcycle comes up along side the truck. Luke, who has been facing the rear the whole time, yells. I see him pointing. His sister pulls off the roof and turns with her rifle.

But Starla is too quick.

Only twenty feet from me, she sidles the crotch rocket up beside the truck and with one leg kicks the side of it with all her monstrous strength. The back tires fly out from underneath the pickup. The truck spins and comes down angled at the woods. When it hits the road again, the tires catch and it hurtles straight off the road and into a tree. There is a hissing crash. Luke and his sister go wheeling into the darkness.

And in one fluid motion, Starla flies by me, reaches out her gigantic paw and scoops me up.

I am whipped into the air. Suddenly I am going 100 mph. She places me behind her on the bike. I grip her back, run my hands through her hair. Smell her body. Home again.

"My hero!" I shout into the wind over the whine of the crotch rocket.

She reaches back and gently fondles my dick with her fingers. "This is not a thing I am willing to leave behind," she says. "There are things in the world worth fighting for, pet."

I smile into her luxurious back. After a few minutes, I ask, "They're not going to stop coming after us are they?"

"No. They are not deceased. I wish it were so, but it is not!" Starla shouts into the oncoming wind.

"Are we going to your homeland?"

"Yes."

"Good," I say, and mean it. After some time, I crawl up her back, so I can see over her shoulder, to watch with Starla as the crotch rocket light illuminates the empty onrushing road before us. I hug my arms around her neck. I kiss her on the cheek. "Where is your homeland, Starla?" I shout. "Please. I want to know."

She points ahead of us, down the road into the dark.

"North?"

"No, look." She points again. Above the oncoming road a full moon is framed by black pine trees.

"The moon?"

"Yes. No. Maybe."

"What?"

"Jay Jason, do you want to know how I am capable of all these endeavors? How I can drive a motorcycle and speak with eloquence and work your shaft and balls like a grade-A pornstar?"

"Yes!" I shout into the hurricane wind, tears whipping from my cheeks into the escaping night. "How!?"

"I am not a Sasquatch," she says, turning her massive head and meeting my gaze with the starlight reflecting in her eyes, "I am not from this world. I am an alien."

The End

ABOUT THE AUTHOR

Well, let me tell you about good ol' Lacey Noonan. Lacey lives on the east coast with her family. When not sailing, sampling fine whiskeys or making veggie tacos, she loves to read and write steamy, strange, silly, psychological and sexy stories. During daylight hours she is a web designer and developer, but mostly a mom.

For more information on Lacey Noonan, why not point your browser snake at:

Amazon Author Profile
amazon.com/author/laceynoonan

Mailing List
http://eepurl.com/bEeNgv

Facebook
facebook.com/laceynoonan123

Twitter
twitter.com/laceynoonan

Email
laceynoonan123@gmail.com

The Wild Ride Continues!

Here, in the long-awaited sequel…

I Don't Care if My Sasquatch Lover Says the World is Exploding, She's Hot But I Play Bass and There's Nothing Hotter Right Now Than Rap-Rock

What would you do if your lady-friend was lying to you?

After narrowly escaping with their lives from the Lemaire family, Jason and Starla are now in a race against time to find the rendezvous point that will get them safely to Starla's homeland.

The fresh air, the free love, the freedom of their Japanese crotch rocket vibrating beneath them... It's a hell of a way to travel.

But something isn't right. Jason suspects Starla doesn't know where she's going. It's obvious she's hiding something important from him. And then one fateful night—just as they're about to make contact with "her people" in a sensual symbiosis of sound at the top of a pine tree—their lives are forever changed... Because that's when Jason abruptly joins Rap-Rock impresarios 311, currently on tour with the Lilith Fair, throwing their whirlwind romance, as well as their lives, into jeopardy.

What's going on? Is it the new millennium or not? Is Jason's wildness getting out of control? Dangerous, even? Is there anything else to eat besides squirrels? Why does Radiohead's new album "Kid A" sound like evil computers sucking down gigabytes of whale dong?

Full of acrobatic writing right up until the stunning conclusion—Lacey Noonan's scintillating turns of phrase that sparkle on the page and dribble off your Kindle with gelatinous joy—this sexy Sasquatch sequel just might be the best thing you read all millennium!

BONUS: Contains a DEFINITIVE LIST of The Top 100 Bands of All-Time that will leave you breathless and panting for more.

Other Books by *Lacey Noonan*

Seduced by the Dad Bod: Book One in the Chill Dad Summer Heat Series

Amanda's back from college for the summer, sexy and bored. Mr. Baldwin is a chill dad who loves swimming, singing '90s hits, Super Soakers and has a body like a big sack of wet sugar. What happens when these two star-crossed lovers cross paths? And oh yeah—he's her boyfriend's dad? Uh-oh! By turns devastatingly erotic and incisive, this first installment of Lacey Noonan's hot new summery Dad Bod saga will leave you questioning everything in your life.

Hot Boxed: How I Found Love on Amazon

Hot Boxed is the story of Randi, a 20-something girl working at an Amazon Distribution Center who wants more out of life. Assuming she'll work there forever, a name pops up on her scanner that ignites her passions. Does she have the courage to break the chains that bind her, to step out of her dreary life and do something so, so, so crazy to get what she wants? Find out in this super-steamy story!

The Babysitter Only Rings Once

This is NOT your typical babysitter story... One night when Sophie realizes she's left something scandalous at the Lindstrom's—the affluent family she has babysat for years now—she goes against all the fibers of her being and decides to get it back—no matter what, even if it means more scandal. Find out what Sophie recovers in this seriously HOT and suspenseful story by Lacey Noonan.

Eat Fresh: Flo, Jan & Wendy and the Five Dollar Footlong

"God damn, marketing events are bitch." And so begins the sexy, wild adventures of our three protagonists, Jan, Flo and Wendy—the three hottest stars of the contemporary TV commercial scene. After a fight with Wendy's agent, the girls take it upstairs to Flo's VIP hotel room, where they soon discover the pleasures of each other's bodies—as well as the very valuable, last remaining Five Dollar Footlong at the event. Caution: Hottt!

A GRONKING TO REMEMBER: BOOK ONE IN THE ROB GRONKOWSKI EROTICA SERIES

Leigh has a serious problem. And it's driving a "spike" between her and her husband Dan. When she accidentally witnesses the NFL's biggest wrecking ball, Rob Gronkowski of the New England Patriots, do his patented "Gronk Spike," she is suddenly hornier than she's ever been. This causes her to go on a rampage of her own—a rampage of "self-discovery." And soon everyone's lives have changed. Romance! Sports!

A GRONKING TO REMEMBER 2: CHAD GOES DEEP IN THE NEUTRAL ZONE (BOOK TWO IN THE ROB GRONKOWSKI EROTICA SERIES)

The saga continues! When Leigh spurns his advances at a party he throws in her honor, Dan's friend Chad kidnaps her, stealing her away to his personal New England Patriots Shangri-La, a secret Man Cave hundreds of feet below sea level he affectionately calls his "Chadmiral's Quarters." There she learns about a side of Gronk she'd never known, changing her life forever. Secrets will be revealed—Gronktastic secrets. Possibly the greatest sequel ever written. Makes the original look like a certified *piece of shit!*

Shipwrecked on the Island of the She-Gods: A South Pacific Trans Sex Adventure

Shipwrecked on the Island of the She-Gods is a seriously sexually-charged adventure of heart-pounding exotica that doesn't skimp on story or skimpily-clad native girls with "a little something extra." And it's a little something extra that Noah, Julian and Owen will experience over and over in the steamy jungle, along the shores and atop towering mountains until they're begging for mercy. And then begging for more

The Hotness: Five Burning Hot Novellas

PREPARE TO BE TURNED THE HELL ON. Here are five novellas that will titillate and drive you wild, running the gamut of erotic fantasies. If you've ever wanted all of Lacey Noonan's books in one easy, accessible place for one low price, then this is the book for you, sexy-pants. Contains the novellas: *Submitting the Landlord; Hot Boxed: How I Found Love on Amazon; The Babysitter Only Rings Once; I Don't Care if My Best Friend's Mom is a Sasquatch, She's Hot and I'm Taking a Shower With Her (…Because It's the New Millennium);* and *Eat Fresh: Flo, Jan & Wendy and the Five Dollar Footlong.*

The Dishes Are Done Man!

Made in United States
Troutdale, OR
12/16/2025